At the Ice Cream Shop

by Kate Anderson

★ Strategy Focus

As you read, think about what might happen at an ice cream shop.

 HOUGHTON MIFFLIN   BOSTON

Story Vocabulary

cone

dish

green

ice cream

kind

napkins

shop

try

wish

I like ice cream.

I like green ice cream.

4

I like the red kind.

I like to try a lot of ice cream.

I like a dish and a cone.

I wish I had napkins!